DEPLOYMENT

One of Our Pieces is Missing

For Jace and Paxton
Love, Julia

The Barry Robinson Center helps children and families where parents serve or have served in the U.S. military.

As a premier non-profit behavioral health system, we offer residential programs for boys and girls, ages 6-17. Children and teens from military-connected families will find a supportive community here. Our programs have been designed to help them find understanding and acceptance, which contributes to their success in treatment. It's our privilege to serve those who have served us.

Visit **www.barryrobinson.org**
or call **1-800-221-1995**

DUPLICATION AND COPYRIGHT

NATIONAL CENTER for
YOUTH ISSUES

6101 Preservation Drive
Chattanooga, TN 37416
www.ncyi.org

ISBN: 978-1937870-47-8 $9.95
Library of Congress Control Number: 2018935820
© 2018 National Center for Youth Issues, Chattanooga, TN
All rights reserved.
Written by: Julia Cook
Illustrations by: Tamara Campeau
Design by: Phillip W. Rodgers
Contributing Editor: Jennifer Deshler
Published by National Center for Youth Issues • Softcover
Printed at Starkey Printing, Chattanooga, Tennessee, U.S.A., April 2018

This is  ME.

And this is the rest of my family.

We all fit together in our family frame.

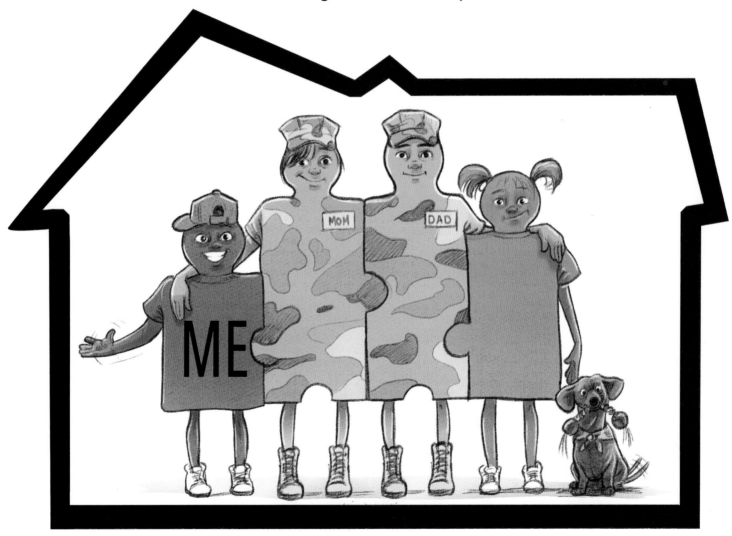

It works because everyone has their own shape and space.

I think I'm pretty lucky because I'm part of a military family.

It makes me really proud to know my parents are working to keep our country safe.

Living the military life is pretty fun for a kid like me!

I get to do stuff other kids don't. My life is kinda unique.

I've tried on night vision goggles and I've looked inside a Humvee.

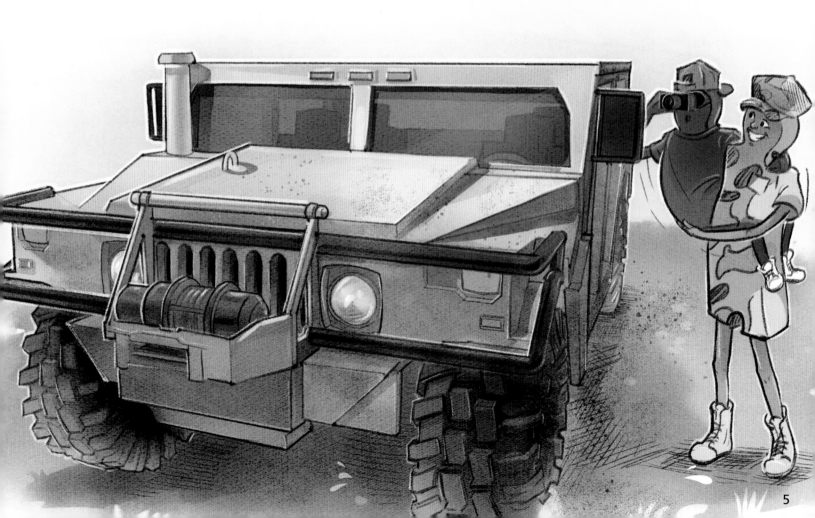

I get to live all over the world.
I have friends in so many places.

I've taken pictures of all of them,
so I'll never forget their faces.

We get to shop at military stores,
that have like a gazillion things.

They even have comic books and candy,
and kites with giant wings!

Oh, and lots of
stuff for dogs, too.

But sometimes, being a military kid isn't that great.

When I move to a different place, my friends can't come with me.
Then, I have to be the new kid again.

And start all over to find different friends,
in a different school, with different teachers…
basically, a different everything.

My dad always tells me, *"Different is change, and change is good, because change always helps you grow."*

The worst part of being a military kid is when one of my parents gets deployed.

That's really hard...

Last year, my dad got deployed. He was excited he got to go.
We all wanted to go with him, But the answer to that was **NO**.

"I'm only going for 200 days, and then I'll be right back home.
We can talk online a lot while I'm gone. And I'll call you on the phone."

"You need to fill in for me while I'm gone, and help your mom out, you know.

Things will be different, but different is change, and change will help you grow."

Before my dad left, our whole family made a paper chain with 200 links in it.

"Every day you can tear off a link. When the chain is gone, I'll be home."

Saying goodbye was *really* hard.

After he left, things weren't the same.
One of our pieces was gone.

"We'll all get through this," my mom said.
"Together we are strong!"

First I was sad.

Then I got mad.

I missed my dad!

I felt so bad.

"I know things are different, but different is change, and change is good, you know.
Don't ever forget what your dad said to you…**Change can help you grow.**"

"We all must change shape to fill in this space, until your dad gets back home.
Everyone will do extra stuff around here, so let's not hear any moans!"

It was my job to feed the dog,

and my sister had to mow the lawn.

But nobody worked as hard as my mom.
She had to be **REALLY** strong.

We all worked so hard to fill the space that was left behind by my dad;
but no matter how hard we worked, changed, and grew, there was
still a missing piece in our family puzzle.

A few months ago when our paper chain was all gone, my dad came back home.

That was the BEST DAY EVER!

I thought things were going to be like they used to be before my dad was deployed…
but they weren't. Everything was different.

When my dad first came home, he tried to get back into our family frame.
But he didn't fit.

We had all grown and changed our shapes to fill in his missing piece.
He had grown and changed, too. He was too big for the space we had for him.

He tried to pound himself in, and it just about broke our frame.
He was different and so were we. Nobody was the same.

He tried so hard to be like before.
But we weren't used to having him there.

And for three straight weeks, our dog was fed twice,
but he certainly didn't care!

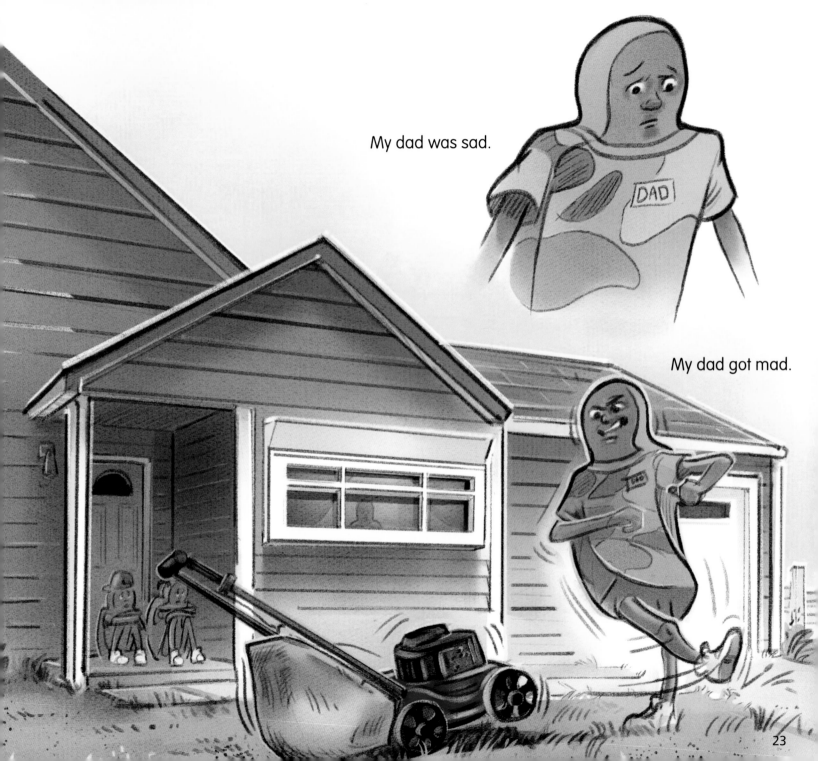

My dad was sad.

My dad got mad.

23

This wasn't my dad.

I felt so bad.

"Everything is so different."

"But dad, that's good, right? Remember, you always told me,
"Different is change, and change is good, because change can help you grow."

You've grown a lot, and so have we.

The next day, we went to a family frame stretcher, because our pieces didn't fit.

She gave us the tools to make our frame bigger, and the courage not to quit.

It took some time, but we all pulled and tugged.
There was so much we all needed to know.

But when we got the things we needed,
our family frame started to grow.

Now our family puzzle looks bigger,
and none of our shapes are the same.

We're happy together, just like before.
And we fit inside of our frame.

I know things are different, but different is change,
and change is good, you know.

I'll never forget what my dad said to me:
Change can help us grow!

Oh, and I still think I'm pretty lucky because I'm part of a military family.

Tips For Helping Kids With Deployment

Deployment can be hard on everyone involved! Changes occur at so many levels when a parent is deployed. When helping kids transition effectively through a deployment, establishing and maintaining Trust and Communication is key.

Here are a few helpful tips:

BEFORE DEPLOYMENT:

- Always answer children's questions as honestly as you can. If you don't know the answer, you can say, "I/we don't know the answer but are doing all we can to make sure everything will be OK," or "I'm not sure, but let me see what I can find out." Then consult others for answers, and follow up with the child. Honest, appropriate information is vital to help children make sense of the situation and maintain trust.

- Address deployment as an honor and a privilege. "When will you get to come home?" "When I'm done helping people."

- Make a family paper chain with links depicting the number of days of deployment (if known) and have children take turns ripping off a link each day. This helps a child conceptualize how long the deployment might last. Other ideas include: chocolate kisses in a jar – a kiss from Mommy every night before bed. Or use a marble jar – take out a marble each day.

- Get twin toy cars (or a similar item) – one for deploying parent to take and one for your child to keep. Take pictures with the cars and share them to help kids feel more connected.

- Record yourself reading books to your kids so they can watch them while you're away.

- Inform teachers/day care providers of deployment so they can plan for providing reassurance at school.

DURING DEPLOYMENT:

- Schedule family meetings throughout the deployment to talk about the "roses and thorns" each family member is dealing with. Talk openly about emotions and discuss changes that may be occurring and how you can work as a family to manage changes. Remember, TRUST and COMMUNICATION are key!

- Stay in touch with teachers/day care providers to ensure you know how your child is doing at school and share any concerns you have.

- Monitor and limit exposure to TV coverage of war efforts.

- Ask family members to visit while your spouse is away to help fill the void.

- Involve children in creating parent care packages on a regular basis.

- Time apart means time to grow. "Won't it be fun to show Dad how you can do _____ when he gets home?"

- Do a fun family study project. Work together to learn about the place of deployment. The more information a child has about where the parent is, the less anxiety will occur.

REINTEGRATION:

- Use the puzzle analogy (or similar concept) to show kids that everyone is now differently shaped and that it will take time to figure out how to fit everyone back into the family frame comfortably. TRUST and COMMUNICATION are key to reintegration.

- As the returning parent, try not to help much during the first week or two. Just observe so you can learn how your family has changed and grown. Then reassure. Remember…go slow to go fast when reintegrating.

- Don't be too proud, afraid or embarrassed to reach out for advice. Deployment and reintegration can be extremely hard on families. You can learn SO much from others who have lived through this experience. You are not alone. Great people and organizations exist to help you and your family through this valuable and challenging experience.